W9-BLJ-799

December Dog

Just then, Pal barked. He tugged on his leash and pulled Bradley toward the shop door.

"It's closed, Pal," Bradley said. "Mrs. Wong isn't here."

Pal barked at a pile of snow outside the door. He climbed over the snow.

Bradley heard a small whimper. He saw two shiny black eyes and a skinny tail wagging back and forth.

"Look at what Pal found!" Bradley cried.

The other kids looked over Bradley's shoulder.

"What is it?" Lucy asked.

"Woof!" the thing in the snow said.

"Jumping jackrabbits!" Nate said. "It's a puppy!"

December Dog

by **Ron Roy**

illustrated by
John Steven Gurney

A STEPPING STONE BOOK™

Random House 🏠 New York

Margaret E. Heggan Public Library
606 Delsea Drive
Sewell, NJ 08080

This is dedicated to kids who read to other kids.
—R.R.

To Kayla and Todd, from Mr. Johnny
—J.S.G.

This is a work of fiction. Names, characters, places, and incidents either are the product of the author's imagination or are used fictitiously. Any resemblance to actual persons, living or dead, events, or locales is entirely coincidental.

Text copyright © 2014 by Ron Roy
Cover art, map, and interior illustrations copyright © 2014 by John Steven Gurney

All rights reserved. Published in the United States by Random House Children's Books, a division of Random House LLC, a Penguin Random House Company, New York.

Random House and the colophon are registered trademarks and A Stepping Stone Book and the colophon are trademarks of Random House LLC.

Visit us on the Web!
ronroy.com
randomhouse.com/kids

Educators and librarians, for a variety of teaching tools, visit us at
RHTeachersLibrarians.com

Library of Congress Cataloging-in-Publication Data
Roy, Ron.
December dog / by Ron Roy ; illustrated by John Steven Gurney.
p. cm. — (Calendar mysteries)
"A Stepping Stone book."
Summary: After finding an unusual present—a lost puppy—on Christmas Eve, best friends Bradley, Brian, Nate, and Lucy scramble to find its owner before morning.
ISBN 978-0-385-37168-1 (trade) — ISBN 978-0-385-37169-8 (lib. bdg.) — ISBN 978-0-385-37170-4 (ebook)
[1. Mystery and detective stories. 2. Dogs—Fiction. 3. Animals—Infancy—Fiction. 4. Christmas—Fiction. 5. Gifts—Fiction.] I. Gurney, John Steven, ill. II. Title.
PZ7.R8139Df 2014 [Fic]—dc23 2013037310

Printed in the United States of America
10 9 8 7 6 5 4 3 2 1

This book has been officially leveled by using the F&P Text Level Gradient™ Leveling System.

Random House Children's Books supports the First Amendment and celebrates the right to read.

Contents

1. It's a Puppy! 1

2. Where Is Mrs. Wong? 7

3. The Nephew 14

4. Where Is Officer Fallon? 23

5. Brian Hears a Splash 29

6. Secret in the Closet 36

7. Clues in the Snow 46

8. Dog-Napper 53

9. Nate Knows Something 60

10. Ellie's Surprise 65

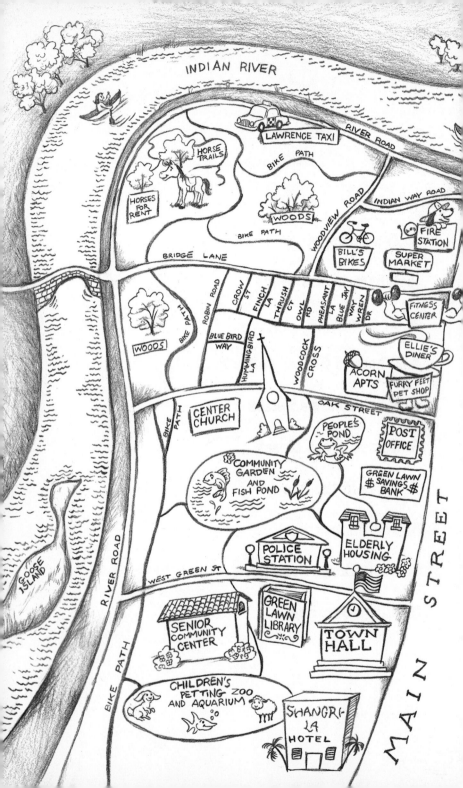

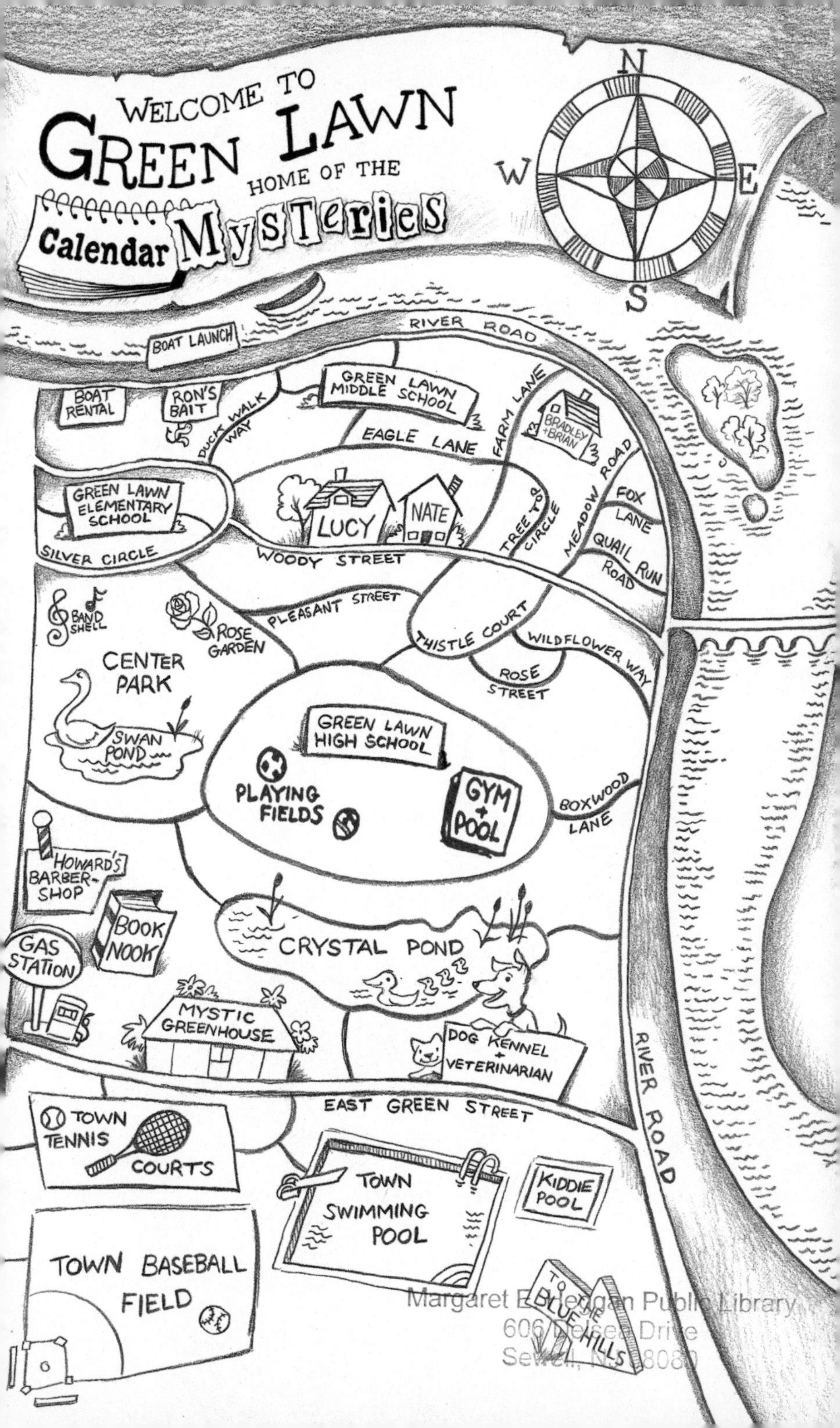

Margaret E. Heggan Public Library
606 Delsea Drive
Sewell, NJ 08080

1
It's a Puppy!

"Let's go see the puppies," Nate said.

"And the Christmas decorations," Lucy added.

It was the afternoon before Christmas. Nate, Lucy, Bradley, and his twin, Brian, were in the twins' yard playing with their basset hound, Pal.

"I can't believe tomorrow morning is Christmas!" Brian said.

Pal barked at Brian.

"Do you think dogs know it's Christmas?" Nate asked.

"He just wants to go for a walk," Brian said.

"Come on, Pal. Want to go see some puppies?" Bradley asked. He snapped Pal's leash on, and the kids started walking toward Main Street in Green Lawn.

The four kids were best friends. Nate's older sister, Ruth Rose, was friends with Lucy's cousin Dink. Bradley and Brian's older brother, Josh, was also pals with Dink and Ruth Rose.

The sun was behind some dark clouds. Snowflakes were falling, beginning to cover last week's snow.

"Yippee, we can have a Christmas snowball fight later!" Brian said. He stuck out his tongue and caught a snowflake.

Main Street was busy. It was Christmas Eve, and some people were still shopping. The parking lot behind the supermarket was crowded. Light poles were decorated with shiny red balls. Christmas carols played from speakers. A plastic Santa sat on top of Ellie's Diner.

"Maybe Mrs. Wong will let us hold the puppies," Nate said.

Mrs. Wong owned Furry Feet, the pet store on Main Street. The kids knew she had puppies up for adoption.

But when they got to Furry Feet, the store window was dark.

The sign was turned off.

"Furry Feet is closed," Lucy said.

The kids put their faces against the cold glass. Pal stood on his hind legs and sniffed the window.

A wooden box stood behind the glass. A few dog toys were scattered around in the box. Food and water bowls sat empty. A big sign on the box said: THE PUPPIES HAVE GONE TO GOOD HOMES. MERRY CHRISTMAS!

Inside the shop were cages of mice, rats, ferrets, and parakeets, and tanks of fish. No puppies.

"Mrs. Wong has found homes for all of them," Nate said.

Bradley thought Nate looked sad. "Maybe you'll get one for Christmas," he said, smiling. He knew that Nate really wanted a puppy.

"No way," Nate said. "Tiger is the only pet my parents will let us have. It's so not fair."

The other three kids knew all about Tiger, Ruth Rose's cat. She was big and sassy and had long, sharp claws.

"I bought Ruth Rose one of those little mechanical mice," Nate went on. "It has a remote so she can make it go all over the house. Tiger will go crazy chasing it!"

"Cool," Bradley said. "Maybe your sister will give you a mechanical dog," he joked.

Nate shook his head. "Probably more socks," he said. "Every year it's socks or mittens."

Just then, Pal barked. He tugged on his leash and pulled Bradley toward the shop door.

"It's closed, Pal," Bradley said. "Mrs. Wong isn't here."

Pal barked at a pile of snow outside the door. He climbed over the snow.

Bradley heard a small whimper. He saw two shiny black eyes and a skinny tail wagging back and forth.

"Look at what Pal found!" Bradley cried.

The other kids looked over Bradley's shoulder.

"What is it?" Lucy asked.

"Woof!" the thing in the snow said.

"Jumping jackrabbits!" Nate said. "It's a puppy!"

2
Where Is Mrs. Wong?

"Oh my gosh!" Bradley said. He picked up the puppy. It shivered in his arms. "How did you get here?"

The puppy was golden brown all over except for its feet. They were white, as if the puppy were wearing four little socks.

Brian, Nate, and Lucy petted the puppy's head. It licked their fingers.

The puppy had a red ribbon tied around its neck. "Look, there's a tag on it!" Lucy said.

She got closer and tried to read what was written on the tag. "It just says *TO* and *FROM*," she said. "The rest is missing."

"Somebody ripped it in half," Brian said.

"Maybe the puppy chewed off the bottom half," Nate suggested.

The puppy was trembling in Bradley's arms. "It's shivering," Bradley said. "Let's take it to my house." He stuck the puppy inside his jacket and zipped it up.

Nate took another look through the window. "I wonder who feeds the animals when Mrs. Wong is on vacation," he said.

"Good question," Lucy said. She rubbed some snow from a corner of the window. A note had been taped to the inside of the glass.

The note said: AWAY UNTIL JAN. 1. FOR EMERGENCIES, CALL 860-555-0505. —MARY WONG

"We should call her," Bradley said. "If someone bought this puppy from Furry Feet, she can tell us who it is!"

"Come on. We can use Ellie's phone," Brian suggested.

"We should write the number down," Nate said.

"No problem," Brian said. He tapped

the side of his head. "I have it locked inside my incredible memory."

Brian took Pal's leash from his brother, and they all trooped over to Ellie's Diner.

"Hey, kids," Ellie said when she saw them. "What are you doing out and about on Christmas Eve?"

"Look what we found in front of Furry Feet!" Bradley said. He unzipped his jacket, and the puppy's head popped out. "It was just curled up there, outside the door."

"For goodness' sake!" Ellie exclaimed. She took the puppy and hugged it against her chest. "Are you hungry, sweetie?"

"Yes," Nate said.

Everyone laughed.

"I meant the puppy," Ellie said. She read the tag. "Gracious, this little guy is supposed to be a Christmas present!"

"That's what we think, too," Lucy said.

Ellie set the puppy on the floor and put a little chopped meat in a dish. The puppy gobbled it up in three seconds.

"I'll give it some of Pal's food when we get home," Bradley said. "But can we borrow a quarter to use your pay phone? Mrs. Wong left a phone number for emergencies. We want to ask her if she knows who adopted the puppy."

"Do you think it was one of the puppies from her store?" Ellie asked.

"We don't know," Brian said. "But that's where it was."

Ellie handed Brian a quarter, and he stepped inside the phone booth. He plunked the quarter into the coin slot and dialed the number he had memorized.

The other kids waited outside the booth, watching Brian talk. He hung up and stepped outside the booth. "It's Mrs. Wong's nephew, Leonard," he said. "He's watching the store while

Margaret E. Heggan Public Library
606 Delsea Drive
Sewell, NJ 08080

she's on vacation. He's coming over."

Ellie poured four mugs of hot chocolate and set them on a table. "Put something warm inside your tummies while
you're waiting," she said.

The kids thanked Ellie and sat down.
They sipped the chocolate and warmed
their hands on the mugs.

"I wonder who's supposed to get the puppy for Christmas," Lucy said.

"Some kid, probably," Nate said. He looked at the clock over Ellie's counter. "And Christmas starts in about eleven hours."

"Maybe it isn't a kid," Brian said. "Maybe some *grandmother* isn't getting a puppy for Christmas."

"So then it's even sadder," Lucy said. "If this puppy is a Christmas present, we have to find out before tomorrow morning!"

3
The Nephew

A tall teenager wearing jeans, a ski jacket, and a baseball cap walked into Ellie's Diner. He came over to their table.

"Is one of you Brian?" the kid asked.

"I am," Brian said. "Are you Leonard Wong?"

"Yup." The kid sat down and pulled off his cap. It was wet with snowflakes.

Leonard looked down at the puppy and Pal, both lying on the floor. "You found this pup outside Aunt Mary's

14

shop?" he asked. He scooped up the puppy and held it in the air. "Cute little guy. It's a boy, by the way."

"He was in a snowbank outside your aunt's store," Brian said. "Our dog found him. We were wondering if your aunt gave him to someone. He has a tag, but it just says *TO* and *FROM*, with no names."

Leonard examined the tag. "Aunt Mary has a picture of the puppies she had," he said. "This guy looks exactly like one of them."

"Awesome!" Bradley said. "So if your aunt had this dog, she must remember who adopted it!"

"And that person might have written the tag!" Nate said.

Leonard pulled a cell phone from his pocket. He pushed a couple of buttons. "Here, ask her," he said. "She's in Florida, scuba diving." He handed the phone to Bradley.

Bradley heard the other phone ringing. Then the ringing stopped. He heard a crackling noise. Bradley could hear static but no voices. He said, "Mrs. Wong? This is Bradley Pinto. Can you hear me?"

He heard more strange noises, and then the phone went silent.

Bradley handed the cell phone back to Leonard. "I couldn't hear anything," he said. "I don't even know if she heard me."

Leonard smiled. "Knowing Aunt Mary, she's underwater," he said. "She's probably taking pictures of fish. Try her again later." Leonard wrote his aunt's cell phone number on a napkin and handed it to Brian.

"So what should we do with the puppy?" Brian asked.

"Don't know, bro," Leonard said, rising from his seat. "But I have to go feed the animals in my aunt's store." He made a face. "And clean all the cages."

Leonard loped out of the diner.

"Let's take the puppy home," Bradley said.

"Wait!" Ellie said. She came over and handed Lucy a bag. The top was tied with a red ribbon. "Merry Christmas!"

The kids thanked Ellie again and headed outside. They stood in front of her diner windows. The snow had almost stopped. Just a few flakes fell from the dark clouds. The kids saw their footprints, and Pal's, in the new snow on the sidewalk.

Pal kept staring at the lump under Bradley's jacket and the bag in Lucy's hands.

People hurried past, carrying bags. Everyone had pink noses. Christmas was in the air!

"What do you think Ellie gave us?" Nate asked.

"Whatever it is, Pal smells it right through the bag," Lucy said.

"Hounds can smell anything a mile away!" Brian said.

"Hey, that gives me an idea," Bradley said. He walked next door to Furry Feet. "Bring Pal over here, Brian."

Bradley aimed Pal's nose toward the spot where the puppy had been lying. Then he opened his jacket so Pal could sniff the puppy's golden fur.

Pal sniffed, then gave the puppy a lick.

"Pal, follow tracks!" Bradley said. "Follow!"

"What are you doing?" Brian asked.

"The puppy must have walked here," Bradley said, zipping his jacket. "Maybe Pal can follow his scent back to wherever he came from!"

"Cool idea!" Nate said.

Pal stuck his nose in the snow and sniffed. Then he pulled Brian back toward Ellie's.

There was an alley between Ellie's Diner and Furry Feet. Pal headed down the alley. The kids followed. At the end of the alley, they passed the Acorn Apartments. Pal kept going, now and then letting out a little bark. He kept his nose on the ground.

Pal stopped near a blue house on Woodcock Cross. He sat and barked at the house.

"Who lives here?" Lucy asked.

"I think it's Officer Fallon's house!" Nate said.

"Does he have a puppy?" Brian asked.

"I don't know," Bradley said, "but if

he does, why was the puppy all the way over on Main Street?"

No one had an answer. The kids let Pal drag them closer to the blue house. The yard and driveway were covered in snow. There were tire tracks leading from the garage. The garage door was open, but there was no car inside.

Brian let Pal off his leash. Pal ran

around and sniffed the snow near the house and driveway. Then he stopped, looked at the kids, and started barking again.

Brian knelt down. "Guys," he said, "Pal found tiny dog tracks in the snow!"

The other kids took a look. Bradley set the puppy on the ground next to the tracks Pal had discovered. He pressed the puppy's feet into the snow, making four new little prints.

The two sets of prints were exactly the same.

"The puppy *did* come from here!" Lucy said.

4
Where Is Officer Fallon?

The kids walked up onto the front porch, and Lucy rang the bell. They heard it chime inside the house. Nobody answered the door.

Bradley looked through a window. "All I see is a Christmas tree," he said. "And the lights are on."

"It's Christmas Eve," Brian said. "Officer Fallon might be Christmas shopping."

"If this *is* his puppy," Bradley said, "maybe Officer Fallon went out looking for him."

Lucy glanced at the other houses along the street. "The puppy could have come from one of those houses," she said. "Just because Pal found the tracks in front of this house doesn't mean the puppy lives here."

"Right," Bradley said. "Maybe he just ran across Officer Fallon's driveway on his way to Main Street."

"We should take him home," Brian said. "He must be hungry."

"Wait a minute. I just thought of something," Nate said. "Jimmy Fallon lives over on Pheasant Lane. That's near here."

"Who's Jimmy Fallon?" Lucy asked.

"Officer Fallon's grandson," Nate said. "If Officer Fallon adopted this puppy from Furry Feet, Jimmy would know it."

"Great idea, Nate! Let's go ask him!" Bradley said.

Nate led the kids and Pal farther down the street. They crossed a dirt road without a name, and turned right onto Pheasant Lane.

"It's the green house," Nate said. "We played soccer over here last summer."

"Let's see if they're home," Brian said.

"But what if the puppy was meant to be a Christmas present to Jimmy from his grandfather?" Bradley asked. "We'll be spoiling the surprise."

"Or maybe Jimmy is giving his grandfather a puppy for Christmas," Nate said. "Only the puppy ran away!"

"Let's find out," Bradley said. He rang the doorbell.

A tall woman wearing a red sweater answered the door.

"Hi, Mrs. Fallon. Is Jimmy home?" Nate asked.

She smiled. "No, I'm afraid not,"

she said. "He's gone off with his grandfather. Some secret mission!"

She looked at the puppy, whose head
was sticking out of Bradley's jacket. "Oh,
how cute," she said. "Is it yours?"

Bradley shook his head. "No, ma'am," he said. "We were wondering if it was Jimmy's. Or Officer Fallon's."

Jimmy Fallon's mom smiled again. "Nope, no puppies live here. And I know Jimmy's grandfather doesn't have one, either."

"Do you think Jimmy was giving the puppy to his grandfather for Christmas?" Lucy asked.

"Goodness, no," Mrs. Fallon said. "I helped pick out Jimmy's gifts for his grandfather. He's getting a new pocket-knife and a wool scarf." She petted the puppy's head. "Do you mean this little tyke is lost?"

The kids all nodded. "We found him on the sidewalk near Furry Feet," Brian said. "We're pretty sure Mrs. Wong gave him to someone. And Pal traced him back to Officer Fallon's house. We saw his tracks in the snow by the driveway!"

"We don't know who he belongs to," Bradley added. "But we think he's supposed to be someone's Christmas present!"

"Goodness, a Christmas mystery," Mrs. Fallon said. "Good luck finding the right owner!"

5
Brian Hears a Splash

The kids thanked Mrs. Fallon and walked back to the sidewalk.

Bradley opened his jacket. He handed the puppy to Nate. "You want to carry him next?"

Nate grinned. "Sure!" He slipped the puppy inside his coat.

They headed back to Main Street. With Pal leading, they hiked past the elementary school to Eagle Lane.

"Can you take the puppy to your house?" Bradley asked Nate.

"I'd like to, but Tiger might have a fit," he said. "So would my mom and my sister!"

"Let's take him to our house," Brian said. "Pal can play with him, so he won't be lonely."

"That's right," Lucy said. "If it hadn't been for Pal's nose, the puppy would still be out in the cold."

The kids walked into the kitchen at Bradley and Brian's house. Bradley saw a note on the table:

> Out shopping.
> See you soon.
> Have a snack.
> —Mom

A bowl of tangerines sat on the table, and the kids each took one. They sat down to peel them.

Nate put the puppy on the floor with Pal and poured some of Pal's food into a

bowl. The puppy raced to the bowl and began eating.

"What should we do with him?" Brian asked, pointing at the puppy's wagging tail.

"We have to find his real home!" Lucy said. "Before tomorrow."

"I know that," Brian said. "I meant right now."

"I'll get a box for him to sleep in," Bradley said.

"What about Mom?" Brian asked, grinning. "She's always telling us, *'No more animals!'*"

Bradley grinned back. "Mom won't find out. We'll hide him, then figure out where the puppy belongs before she even knows he's here."

"But *how* are we going to figure it out?" Nate asked. "*TO* and *FROM* are still a mystery."

"I'll try calling Mrs. Wong again," Brian said. "If the puppy came from her shop, she can tell us who adopted him. If she does, we'll just bring the puppy where he belongs. Mystery solved!"

Brian pulled the napkin from his back pocket. "Leonard wrote the number down."

He dialed the number. "It's ringing," he whispered to the kids in the kitchen.

Then he said, "Hello, Mrs. Wong? This is Brian Pinto in Green Lawn. We found a puppy, and we think it came from your store! We're trying to find—"

Brian held the phone away from his ear and looked at it.

Then he put it back to his ear. "Mrs. Wong? Are you there?"

Brian hung up.

"What happened?" Bradley asked.

"I heard a splash," Brian said. "Then nothing."

"Maybe she jumped into the water," Lucy said.

"Or she dropped her cell phone in the water," Bradley suggested.

"She's scuba diving!" Nate said. "Maybe a shark swallowed Mrs. Wong *and* her cell phone!"

The four kids looked at each other. "We have to hide the puppy before Mom and Dad get home," Bradley said.

"Maybe we should walk around town and ask everybody we see if they lost a puppy," Lucy said.

"Let's call the police station," Brian said. He was still standing next to the phone. "If someone lost this little guy, they might have reported it."

"Good idea!" Lucy said. "In my hometown, the police have a special officer in charge of finding lost pets."

Brian dialed the police station. "This is Brian Pinto," he said into the phone. "My friends and I found a puppy on Main Street. Do you know if anybody lost one?"

Brian listened. "We brought him home," he said. "On Farm Lane."

He listened again. "He might be a Christmas present for someone," he said. He explained about the tag.

"Okay, we will. Thank you," Brian said before he hung up.

"We will what?" Bradley asked his twin.

"The dispatcher says we should put pictures of the puppy on telephone poles and in stores," Brian said.

"On Christmas Eve?" Nate asked. He looked out the window. "It's snowing again, and it'll be dark pretty soon."

Lucy nodded. "People are sitting around their Christmas trees," she said. "No one's out looking at telephone poles!"

They all gazed at the puppy, curled up on the rug next to Pal. "I guess we keep him till Mrs. Wong gets back from Florida," Bradley said.

"You mean *if* she gets back," Nate said. "She might be in a shark's belly!"

Bradley sighed. "I'll look in the basement for a box," he said.

6

Secret in the Closet

The kids carried the box up to Bradley and Brian's bedroom and closed the door. "Let's put it in the closet so snoopy Josh doesn't see the puppy," Bradley said.

They moved some stuff and made room for the box on the closet floor. Brian put one of his old sweatshirts in the box so the puppy would have something soft to lie on. Bradley added one of Pal's toys and a bowl of water.

They set the puppy in the box and

watched him lap up some water.

"He needs a name," Nate said.

"He's so cute, we should call him Brian," Brian said. He grinned.

"Whoever is getting him for Christmas should name him," Bradley said. "Not you, cute brother."

"And he might already have a name," Lucy said.

Just then, the kids heard a door slam. "It's Mom and Dad!" Brian whispered. "We'd better get out of here before they come upstairs!"

"Be a good boy," Bradley whispered to the puppy as he closed the closet door, leaving it open a crack.

The four kids walked down the stairs and into the kitchen.

"Hi, gang," Bradley's dad said. "What mischief are you up to?"

"We're bored with all this snow," Brian told his father. "So we're going to

Hawaii. Can we borrow your car?"

"Sure," his father said. "When you're thirty-five."

"Do you want to stay for popcorn and hot chocolate?" Bradley's mother asked Nate and Lucy.

"No thank you, Mrs. Pinto," Lucy said. "I have to go call my parents in Arizona."

"And I get to open one of my presents," Nate said. "Probably some new underwear or more socks."

Nate and Lucy left through the back door.

"Okay, who wants popcorn?" Bradley's mom asked.

Just then, they heard a bark from upstairs.

Bradley looked at Brian. Brian's eyes grew big.

"Maybe Pal got locked in our room," Bradley said. "I'll go up and get him."

But Pal walked into the kitchen.

"I thought he was upstairs," Bradley's father said.

"I guess not," Bradley said. He was thinking, *Quiet, puppy!*

"I could swear I heard a bark from up there," Bradley's mother said.

"Maybe it was Josh," Brian offered. "He makes a lot of funny noises."

"Josh is out somewhere with Dink and Ruth Rose," his dad said. "And I've never heard him bark."

"I thought we were having popcorn," Brian said.

"And hot chocolate!" Bradley said. "Yum, yum!"

While their parents were making the popcorn and hot chocolate, Bradley and Brian high-fived.

Ten minutes later, Bradley's father carried the tray into the living room. They sat in front of the Christmas tree.

"Mom, can we open one present now?" Brian asked.

"I don't know, honey," his mother said. "Christmas is tomorrow."

"Pretty please?" Brian begged. "Just a tiny present."

"I guess it will be all right," their mother said. "Take those two flat ones in the striped paper."

"Hey, if the twins get to open something, I do, too!" their father said.

Just then, Josh burst into the room. "Me too!" he said.

"I thought you were with Dink and Ruth Rose," his mother said.

"They had to do some stuff," Josh said. "Christmas stuff."

"You look funny," Josh's father said. "Why is your face red?"

"Do you have a temperature?" his mother asked. She put her hand on Josh's forehead.

"I'm okay. I ran home," Josh said. Then he reached for a present with his name on it. "Can I open this one?"

"Sure," his father said. "But let the twins open theirs first, please."

Bradley and Brian tore the striped paper off. They each found a book.

Bradley's book was called *Swamp Secrets*. Brian's was *100 Amazing Magic Tricks*.

"Cool," Brian said. "Come on, Brad. Let's go up to our room and read. When we finish, we can swap books!"

"No!" Josh yelled.

The twins stared at their big brother. "Why not?" Bradley asked.

"Because I haven't opened *my* present yet," Josh said. He held the present on his lap. He read the tag. *"To Josh, from Mom and Dad."*

Josh grinned. "Thanks, parents." He shook the present. "It's heavy," he said.

"Are you going to open it or not?" Brian asked.

Slowly, Josh removed the paper. Inside he found a toolbox filled with tools.

"So you can fix your own bike," his father said.

"Awesome!" Josh said. "Thanks so much, you guys."

"Can we go up and read now?" Bradley said.

"No!" Josh said. "Let's sing some Christmas carols!"

"Carols?" his mother said. "You've always hated singing carols. Maybe you *are* coming down with something."

They heard a door slam.

"Who was that?" Bradley's father asked. "We're all here."

Josh looked toward the kitchen. "I must have left the back door open," he said.

"So who just closed it?" his mother asked.

"The wind, I guess," Josh said.

"I think that was the front door," Bradley said.

"There are a lot of strange noises in this house today," his father said.

"Maybe it's a ghost," Brian joked.

"Go on up and read," the twins' father said. "Enjoy your books."

Bradley and Brian raced up the stairs. Their bedroom door was open.

"I thought we closed it," Brian whispered.

The closet door was open, too. All the way.

The box was tipped over, and they didn't see the puppy.

"Oh no!" Bradley cried. "Where is he?"

They searched the closet, under the bed, and outside in the hallway. They even checked Josh's room and their parents' room.

The puppy was gone.

"He ran away again!" Brian said.

7

Clues in the Snow

Bradley grabbed a jacket and tossed Brian his. "Come on. Maybe he went back to Furry Feet!"

The twins ran down the stairs.

"Where are you guys going?" their father asked. "I thought you wanted to read your new books."

Bradley grinned. "Um, we need to see about another Christmas present," he said. "A very important one!"

The twins put on their boots, mittens, and hats, and raced out the door. Snowflakes got in their eyes as they ran. They went the shortest way, through Center Park. Swan Pond was frozen over. Snow covered the ice and trees, making the whole park look like a Christmas card.

Five minutes later, Bradley and Brian were in front of Furry Feet.

"Please let him be here," Bradley said, out of breath.

But there was only snow in front of the pet shop. They peered through the glass. Inside, the shop was still dark. Only the fish tanks were lit. The hamsters, ferrets, and mice were sleeping.

"Where could the puppy be?" Brian said.

Bradley looked up and down Main Street. "We have to find him or he'll freeze!" he said.

Brian looked at the snow-covered sidewalk. "Do you see any tracks?" he asked.

"Only ours," Bradley said. He pointed to their footprints crossing Main Street and Center Park. "No puppy prints at all."

"Oh my gosh!" Brian said. "We should have looked for the puppy's tracks outside our house. Maybe we can follow his trail!"

The boys raced away, heading back home. They charged across Center Park, following their own trail.

A few minutes later, they were in their front yard, searching for puppy tracks. They didn't see any, but they did see a lot of human tracks in the yard and on the porch. The twins stood over the tracks.

"Boot prints," Brian said. "But they're not from us. These are bigger."

"And we came out the back door," Bradley added. "We didn't even walk here. But Josh was out here. Maybe they're his."

Brian shook his head. "These aren't Josh's prints, either," he said. "He came in the back door, too. Mom always makes us come in the back way so we can take off our boots."

"So whose tracks are these?" Brian asked. He pointed at two different boot prints, one bigger than the other.

"Oh my gosh!" Bradley said. "Maybe the puppy didn't run away. Maybe he got kidnapped, and these are the kidnappers' footprints!"

"And maybe that's why the puppy barked!" Brian said.

"And when we heard the door slam, that was the kidnappers leaving!" Bradley added.

"They must have come in the front door and snuck up the stairs while we were opening our presents," Brian said. "The kidnappers walked right past us!"

"Maybe they left some clues in our room!" Bradley said.

The boys raced around the house and slammed through the back door.

"Boots off, please!" the twins' mother called from the living room.

They kicked off their boots, ran through the kitchen, and started up the stairs in their socks.

"Did you take care of your very important Christmas present so soon?" their father called.

"Almost!" Bradley said as they shot up the stairs.

They ran into their room. It was the same as they'd left it. The puppy's box was on its side, next to the water bowl. The closet door and bedroom door were still open.

The boys looked around the room with detectives' eyes. "I don't see any clues," Brian said.

"I do," Bradley said. "There's water in the bowl."

"Why wouldn't there be?" Brian asked. "We filled it when we put the puppy in the box."

"But, Brian, if the puppy had tipped the box over, the water would have spilled onto the floor," Bradley said. "If a kidnapper *stole* the puppy, they probably wouldn't spill the water out of the bowl."

"Look!" Brian said. He was on his knees, pointing to something on the rug near the door.

Bradley knelt next to his brother. "It's only snow," he offered. "We just came in from outside."

"Dude, we took off our boots downstairs!" Brian said. "But this is a footprint. Check out those little squares of snow, like a waffle. And that round part is the heel. This snow came off the bottom of someone's boot!"

"Someone who *didn't* take their boots off before they came upstairs," Bradley whispered. *"A dog-napper!"*

8
Dog-Napper

"We have to tell Officer Fallon!" Brian said.

"We tried before, and he's gone somewhere with Jimmy, remember?" Bradley said.

"Then I'm calling Nate and Lucy," Brian went on. He tiptoed out of the room. Two minutes later, he was back. "They're coming over."

"I can't believe someone snuck in here and stole the puppy," Bradley said. "Besides Nate and Lucy, who else even knows we found him?"

"That guy Leonard," Brian said. "And Ellie. Oh, and whoever I talked to at the police station."

Bradley nodded. "And don't forget we told Jimmy Fallon's mom," he said.

"So those four people knew we had the puppy," Brian said. "But why would any of them steal him?"

Brian sat on his bed. "Maybe he's worth a million dollars!" he said. "Maybe he's a famous dog on TV or in the movies!"

Bradley grinned. "Bro, he's just a baby puppy," he said. "He's too young to be famous."

"Well, someone took him, and this is totally a clue!" Brian said, pointing to the clump of boot snow. He slid a sheet of drawing paper under the clump, folded the paper carefully, and ran out of the room.

Bradley thought about a dog-napper

sneaking into their house. Maybe the person wore a ski mask! He got goose bumps.

Brian burst back into the room. "I put the snow in the freezer," he said.

"Why?" Bradley asked.

"In case we need it to show Officer Fallon," Brian said. "When we catch the bad guy!"

"What bad guy?" Nate asked as he and Lucy walked into the room. They were still wearing their jackets.

"How'd you get in?" Brian asked. "We didn't hear you."

"Josh let us in," Lucy said. "He was heading over to Dink's when we got here. Your mom made us take off our boots."

"It's a house rule," Bradley said.

"What bad guy?" Nate asked again.

"And why wouldn't you tell us anything on the phone?" Lucy asked Brian.

"You said it was an emergency."

"WHAT BAD GUY?" Nate asked for the third time.

Bradley opened the closet door. "The bad guy who stole the puppy," he said.

Nate and Lucy stared at the empty box.

"Someone stole the puppy!" Nate yelped.

"When did it happen?" Lucy finally asked. "We just left him in the closet a little while ago!"

Bradley explained how they'd been downstairs eating popcorn and opening presents. "We didn't see or hear any-body," he said.

"We heard the puppy bark," Brian said. "And we heard a door slam. Then when we came back up here, he was gone!"

"Maybe he just ran away, like last time," Lucy said.

"No way," Brian said. "We found a clue. There was snow in our room!"

"Snow?" Nate asked. "Why is that a clue?"

"Snow from the bottom of someone's boot, and it wasn't ours!" Bradley said. "We're going to show it to Officer Fallon, if we ever find him!"

Nate looked around the room. "Show him the snow? Won't it melt?" he asked.

Brian grinned. "I put it in the freezer downstairs."

"You think whoever took the puppy left the snow?" Lucy asked. "How will it help Officer Fallon find the crook?"

"It's in a pattern," Brian explained. "Little shapes like you see on the bottom of boots and sneakers. Detectives on TV check out the soles of shoes and boots all the time!"

"My boots have little triangles on the bottom," Lucy said.

"Brian's and mine have zigzags,"
Bradley said.

"Can you show us the snow?" Nate
asked Brian.

"Sure. Let's go downstairs," Brian
said.

In their stocking feet, the four kids crept down the stairs. They could hear Christmas music coming from the living room. In the kitchen, Brian opened the freezer. He carefully pulled the folded drawing paper from behind some frozen peas.

"Just take a quick peek," Brian said. "I don't want it to melt."

He unfolded the paper. The four kids stared at the boot print. They saw a bunch of squares of snow. Anyone could tell it came off the bottom of someone's shoe or boot.

Nate started to laugh. "Dude, that's no dog-napper. That came from my sister's boot. She leaves clumps just like this all over our kitchen floor."

9
Nate Knows Something

"Your sister?" Brian said. "Ruth Rose?"

"I only have one sister," Nate said. He pointed to a small circle in the middle of one of the squares of snow. "See that? That's a thumbtack in the bottom of her boot. I saw it there this morning."

"Are you sure?" Bradley asked.

"Positive," Nate said. "If we go home, I'll show you."

"Ruth Rose snuck into our room?" Bradley said.

Brian slid the paper back into the

freezer. "Why would she steal our puppy?" he asked.

Nate shrugged. "Maybe she didn't. There's no puppy in my house," he said. "Just one big cat with sharp claws."

"I can't believe she'd take the puppy," Bradley said. "She's our friend!"

"Bro, we know Ruth Rose was in our room, and the puppy is gone. Who else could have taken it?" asked Brian.

"Let's go talk to her," Nate said. "I think she's at Dink's house."

Bradley and Brian grabbed their jackets from the hallway.

"Going for a walk, Mom!" Bradley yelled into the living room.

"Take your dog," their father called.

Bradley looked at the other three kids. "Do they know about . . . ?" he whispered.

"Dad means take Pal," Brian whispered back. He called, "Here, Pal!"

Pal came bounding to Brian, and he clipped on the dog's leash. They stepped outside and started walking. Pal sniffed the fresh snow.

The houses on Farm Lane looked pretty. The roofs were covered with snow, and the kids could see Christmas trees through some windows. A man was out walking his dog. The dog was a greyhound, and it had a red scarf wrapped around its long neck. The two dogs woofed at each other.

At the corner of Farm Lane and Woody Street, they turned right and came to Nate's house. He looked up and pointed.

"That's Ruth Rose's room, but her light isn't on. She must be next door."

The kids trudged to Dink's house. A lot of lights were on. Lucy opened the door, and they all hung up their jackets and kicked off their boots.

Nate picked up a blue boot from the pile under the coatrack. "This is my sister's," he said. He turned the boot over. Stuck in the sole was a thumbtack.

"Same little squares," Brian said. "The frozen clue came from this boot!"

Dink's mother came out of the kitchen. "Hi, kids," she said. She bent and patted Pal's head. "Merry Christmas, Pal!"

"Hi, Mrs. Duncan," the kids said.

"Is my sister here?" Nate asked.

Mrs. Duncan nodded. "She and Josh are up in Dink's room with the door closed." She smiled. "Some big Christmas secret, they told me. Here, Lucy, take these up with you." She handed a plate of cookies to Lucy.

The four kids climbed the stairs, with Pal leading the way. They walked down the hall to Dink's room. The door was closed. They heard music and laughing from inside the room.

Lucy knocked. "Dink, it's Lucy," she said. "Your mom sent up some cookies."

The door opened, but not all the way. Josh's face peered out. "I'll take them," he said. One of his arms came through the opening to grab the plate.

Before the door could close, a golden-brown puppy with white feet shot through the opening.

10
Ellie's Surprise

A lot of things happened at once:

Pal barked at the puppy.

Bradley grabbed the puppy.

The door slammed shut.

The puppy licked Bradley's face.

Whispering came from behind Dink's bedroom door.

Then the door opened again. "Come on in," Dink said.

Bradley, Brian, Nate, Lucy, and Pal walked into Dink's room. Josh was sprawled on Dink's bed. Ruth Rose sat on the other. Dink went and sat on the floor under a cage. Dink's guinea pig, Loretta, was in the cage, standing on her hind legs.

"Um, I took the puppy from your room," Ruth Rose said.

"And I helped her," Dink said. "We snuck upstairs while all you guys were in the living room."

"We know," Brian said. "I found some snow from Ruth Rose's boot."

"Why did you take our puppy?" Bradley asked. The puppy licked his chin.

"He's not your puppy," Ruth Rose said. "He's mine. I got him from Mrs. Wong two days ago."

"You adopted a puppy?" Nate asked his sister. "But you already have a cat!"

Ruth Rose grinned at Nate. "The puppy is for you," she said. "Merry Christmas, little bro."

Nate blinked. "You got me a puppy?"

Ruth Rose nodded. She had a big grin on her face.

Nate ran across the room and gave Ruth Rose a hug.

Dink, Josh, and Ruth Rose were smiling.

Bradley handed the puppy to Nate.

"But we found him in the snow, in front of Furry Feet," Bradley said. "How did he get there?"

Ruth Rose made room for Nate and the puppy next to her on the bed. "Dink and Josh and I went into Mrs. Wong's store to find you a puppy," she said. "Officer Fallon and Jimmy were there, looking at the ferrets."

"They knew you got a puppy?" Brian asked.

Ruth Rose nodded. "I picked this one because of his feet looking like socks. I always give Nate socks for Christmas! But I knew if I brought the puppy home, Nate would find out," she said. "I asked Mrs. Wong if I could leave the puppy in her store until Christmas morning. But she said no—she was going to Florida."

"We tried to call her," Bradley said.

"Anyway, Officer Fallon said *he'd* keep the puppy and bring it to our house on Christmas morning," Ruth Rose went on.

"But then Officer Fallon called us

and said the puppy ran away," Dink said. "He and Jimmy went out looking for it. So did Josh and Ruth Rose and I."

"But how did you know *we* found the puppy?" Lucy asked.

Ruth Rose laughed. "Nate told us," she said. "He came home when Dink and Josh and I were getting ready to go out searching again."

"Oh my gosh, you're right!" Nate said. "I just ran in and said, 'We found a puppy outside Mrs. Wong's and it's at Bradley and Brian's house!'"

Ruth Rose nudged her brother. "I almost told you the truth about the puppy right then," she said. "But I decided to wait till Christmas."

"Then we called Officer Fallon so he wouldn't worry," Josh said.

"And we made a plan to have Dink and me sneak up to Bradley and Brian's room and get the puppy," Ruth Rose said to her brother. "I wanted to give him to you on Christmas morning."

"So when we heard the door slam, that was you and Dink leaving with the puppy?" Bradley asked.

Ruth Rose nodded.

"My job was keeping the family busy downstairs," Josh said. "And it worked!"

Pal put his big paws on Nate's knees and licked the puppy's foot. Nate set the puppy on the floor, and the two dogs sniffed each other.

"This is the best present I ever got for Christmas," he said. "I'm naming him Socks!"

Lucy jumped up. "Oh, I just remembered something!"

She hurried out of the room, and they could hear her running down the stairs. A minute later, she ran back up the stairs.

She came into the room holding a paper bag tied with a red ribbon. "It's a

present from Ellie, remember?"

Lucy untied the ribbon and looked inside the bag. Then she laughed and pulled out a cookie. It was in the shape of a puppy. Ellie had put white frosting on the four feet.

Brian grabbed the bag and poured out the rest of the cookies. Each one was a brown puppy with white feet. He took a big bite of one.

Then he spit it out as fast as he could. "Yuck! That tastes awful!"

A small white card was in the bag
with the cookies. Lucy read the note out
loud: "To New Puppy + Pal: Enjoy my
special doggy cookies. Merry Christmas
from Ellie."